Trauma Drama

Doreen Ngemera

Tried and Trusted
Indie Publishing

Edited by
Gary Smailes - BubbleCow

Cover design by
Sally's Studio
Design and illustration

Illustrations by
Jordan Thatcher

Emoticons
(c) Canstock Photo Inc./cougarsan

For permission requests, address the request to the author c/o
Doreen Ngemera
dorngemera@gmail.com

Visit Doreen Ngemera on Youtube

Tried And Trusted
Indie Publishing
PO Box 2728
Rowville, Victoria, 3178
www.tatindiepublishing.com.au
triedandtrustedindie@gmail.com

To my family

ACKNOWLEDGEMENTS

For this book to become a success, of course some people had to chip in...

Onto the person who always motivated me to keep on writing until I reached the end – my dad, Mwemezi. Without him I might have either ended up halfway, or reached the end like I have, with a bit of a struggle here and there. Hey! I can't predict the future. Another thing, I really appreciate the time he spared to review my book with me, even if it meant staying up on countless nights. I know, I know, sleep is important guys.

Apart from spending sleepless nights, my mom, Cecilia also took part in my book's journey. She advised me of the areas where I could improve, since after all there has to be improvements here and there.

My siblings, Ethan and Petra helped a lot by being my general advisors – giving me their creative views on things from my book's title to the book cover. With them, I don't want to leave out two of my friends, Claire and Lizzy who also chipped in with their ideas regarding my book cover.

I would also like to recognize my teachers and instructors at Feza International School and The Latham School for inspiring me to get into creative writing.

Next is Gary Smailes and Jordan Thatcher. Jordan for bringing Alize's character to life with his illustrations, which amazed me every time I saw them, And Gary for inspecting every little detail of our friend Alize's diary.

Last but not least, Margaret Gregory. She was the one who put Alize's story and the illustrations together to be made into the amazing book that it is today.

BEFORE YOU GO ON WITH THE BOOK, YOU
HAVE TO SIGN A CONTRACT TO PROMISE
THAT IF YOU ARE EVER LUCKY TO MEET MY
MOM (ALICE ADLER) YOU WILL NOT
MENTION THE TOP SECRETS IN THIS BOOK!

GOT IT?

IF YOU ARE READY, SIGN THE CONTRACT
BELOW...

I,

X _______________________________________
Name

PROMISE NOT SPILL ANY OF ALIZE'S
SECRETS TO ANYONE, EVER, ESPECIALLY TO
HER MOM. I WILL KEEP MY PROMISE AND
STICK TO THE RULES...

X _______________________________________
Signature

Before you read any further into this book I'd like to tell you it was NOT my choice to write in here.

This isn't even a book, but a diary, as you could tell from the front cover. That's the reason why I don't want to write in here. I just feel like diaries aren't my thing.

Well, I wasn't entirely forced to write in this ~~book~~ diary but my mom kept on insisting. She thinks that I need this since I am starting middle school and middle school can be quite dramatic and all that.

Getting me this diary was very thoughtful of her, but I don't really think I need this and, as I said, I'm not the kind of person who would normally write in a diary.

I am going to stop writing right now. I promised myself that I wouldn't write in this ~~book~~, I mean diary, EVER, except for this short intro.

NOTE TO SELF:

DON'T TOUCH THIS BOOK EVER AND JUST
BURN IT IF POSSIBLE

CHANGE IN PLANS

Okay, I said I wasn't going to write in this diary. Well, I obviously changed my mind.

I have realized that maybe my mom was right about this diary. I really do need it because my life has already taken a drastic turn. That is even before school has started.

Can you believe that?

Another reason is that if I write in this diary maybe I could print out some copies and, you know, make money and become famous. I would love that. BUT, who would want to read someone else's diary, especially this one since my life is always boring?

So, when I say something dramatic has happened don't get all excited. Trust me on this one or else you will end up getting disappointed.
Let's get on with this "diary".

I just remembered something.

I DIDN'T INTRODUCE MYSELF.

Some of you might have been wondering who I am. Honestly I can't believe I forgot to introduce myself. It's like the most important part.

Below is a fact file about me. As you'll see, I am not a very exciting person.

FIRST NAME	ALIZE
MIDDLE NAME	McStink
LAST NAME	ADLER
AGE	13
FAMILY FACTS	Four in my family; my parents and my annoying six-year-old sister.
SCHOOL	SOUTH EAST MIDDLE SCHOOL(SEMS).
FRIENDS	NONE (Used to have one but she betrayed me, will explain our history later on.)
LIKES	FOOD, BOOKS, SLEEP, MOVIES, MUSIC.
DISLIKES	SPORTS.

Now that I am done with that we can finally move on. And yes my middle name is McStink. I never wanted anyone to know but that was until my so called best friend changed it. That is a story I will tell later on.

Remember when I said I came back to this diary because something dramatic happened? Well, I will explain about that.

UNEXPECTED NEIGHBORS

It was a normal Saturday morning. I woke up, got ready and went downstairs for breakfast.

My mom was baking cake and some cookies. To be honest, I was taken by surprise because she is never awake this early, especially on a Saturday morning.

"Mom why are you baking cookies?" I asked her.

"Oh Nathan, should we tell her?" she asked my dad.

She seemed excited for some reason.

"No, she'll have to find out by herself when she takes the cookies to them," my dad answered with a big grin across his face.

"Please tell me Dad," I asked.

"Fine, but all I can say is that we have new neighbors who moved in yesterday," he said looking at my mom.

"Really! That's great but why are you guys so excited?" I asked.

"Now you will have to find that out when you take these cookies to them," my mom said.

Something weird was going on.

I decided not to ask any more questions since I wouldn't get answers in the end.

I had cereal and some of the cookies my mom made with milk. I had to admit the cookies were good. I enjoyed every bit of it's savory taste till I finished it.

After taking my breakfast, it was time to find out what was so special about the people my parents were so hyped up about.

I was just about to leave when my sister, Amanda, came rushing down the stairs.

"Alize! ALIZE!" she screamed.

"Amanda don't tell her," my mom warned her.

"Why?" she asked.

"It's a surprise for her," my dad told her.

"Oh okay," she said with a sly grin across her face looking at me.

After the bizarre interaction I had with my family, questions raced across my mind as I couldn't take the curiosity any longer! I wanted to know who the new neighbors were. And how they became so special that my family was on and off about them.

I decided to head out and a couple of seconds later, I was at the new neighbor's front door. Just as I was about to ring the bell something in the backyard caught my attention. I backed up from the door and went to have a look in the backyard.

I saw a car.

Now what's so special about seeing a car? You might ask.

Well, this was a FAMILIAR car.

I'd known some people who had one just like it. I hoped it didn't belong to those people.

I definitely hoped not, but my parents had been behaving really oddly.

TRIP TO MEMORY LANE

Okay guys, I don't want to get ahead of myself, but I will explain about all this shortly.

You see, it can't possibly be them.

They moved out of town.

I decided I needed to chill, so I took a couple of deep breaths and thought for a moment. Most likely, the car belonged to some nice people and it was coincidence that it looked the same.

However the sum where my parents were so hyped up, definitely did not add up to that new and positive perception.

Not wanting to waste more time than I already had, I gathered up my courage to walk back and ring the doorbell.

No one came to answer the door after I rang it a few times so I decided it was best if I left. Besides I would have the cookies to myself.

Then again just as I was about to give up and leave, the door opened.

The person who opened the door caused lots of terrifying memories to flash through my mind. I felt as weak as if I had seen a ghost. It took all my strength not to just give in and cry. I wondered if my mind was playing tricks on me.

I didn't want to believe that the person who opened the door was one of my new neighbors.

"Maddie who's at the door?" her mom asked from inside the house.

She didn't answer. I guess she was also speechless. We both just stood there staring at each other. I had mixed emotions bottled up inside of me at that moment.

Her mom came to the door.

"Oh Alize you're here. Look at you all grown up," she said to me.

I faked a smile and really hoped she bought it. She didn't know what had happened between Maddie and me.

Before all of you get different ideas on what really happened to me and Maddie, let me just explain.

The incident happened not long ago; two years ago, when we were both in fifth grade.

Maddie and I were best friends at the time. Mind you we had known each other for a very long time. Maddie and I actually first met on our first day of kindergarten. Since that day we became best friends. We were inseparable.

We were so close, we shared all our secrets and that is how she came to know a secret I've always liked to keep from people. That secret was my middle name- McStink. I know I shouldn't be ashamed of the name which I'm not anymore but was back in those days when I was younger.

Anyway I knew I could always trust her.

All that changed when Maddie revealed to everyone in our grade that my middle name was McStink. She knew how I felt about the name and that I wanted no one to know about it so she promised me that it would stay between us.

That wasn't even the worst part, she also spread lies saying that I was always talking behind people's backs and made up fake stories about them.

I had always wondered the reason for what she did, but the conclusion I've come up with was jealousy. She was jealous of me. You know it was funny to think that she could ever be jealous of me.

So, you know what guys, **never** let haters **stop** you in any way. Instead use them as a **motivation** to keep you going.

Over these past two years I had to live up with people giving me nicknames like 'stinky' and whenever I walked by in the hallways at school most people would scrunch up their noses and say, 'Eww, what's that smell', or 'Oh stinky Alize is here'.

I know most of you are probably thinking that I should have told my parents about this Maddie incident but I didn't. I don't know why and I regret not doing so now. Both our parents think we are still best friends - but if only they knew.

Those were the most painful last years of elementary and it was all because of Maddie. Now just as everything was going back to normal and I moved schools she just pops up back in town.

What a way to start a new school, am I right?

That is why I realized that using this diary really helps. I can jot down my thoughts and how I feel about everything else that happens.

Just like with my "new" neighbors.

Anyway back to the moment I was at.

I was standing there trying to fake a smile because I didn't want her mom to know something was wrong.

"Why don't you come in Alize?" her mom asked.

"No its okay I was just about to leave anyway," I said.

"Okay, well next time then and why aren't you two talking? Don't you need to catch up on stuff?" she asked us.

"Mom we can do that later, right Alize?" Maddie reassured her mom.

"Yeah, we can! Well bye, Maddie," I said trying to sound enthusiastic.

After exchanging all the goodbyes, I was finally out of there. OMG! I think that was the worst moment of my life this year. There was too much pretending and fake smiles that I felt like I wouldn't survive. For real. The thought of what happened back then still gives me goosebumps.

Right now, I just don't want to see her ever again but that wish was definitely not coming true. Just as things were going fine in my life, she just comes back in. Like seriously?

WHY DOES THE UNIVERSE HATE ME?!

THE MALL

Today, I woke up feeling thrilled about the day. My mom was taking me shopping. It felt like I hadn't got new clothes in like forever and my wardrobe surely needed an upgrade.

There was a bad part to it though, but even after finding out that I had would have to watch my little sister, Amanda, my mood was still in sync. I was supposed to take no more than thirty minutes to do my shopping as my mom had to do some grocery shopping afterwards, which was why I was to watch Amanda.

We left the house when we were all ready and took off to the mall. The whole ride there, I was hoping that I wouldn't run into anyone. Maddie to be more specific.

My mom gave me some money for shopping when we'd arrived at the mall. It was enough for me as I didn't want to buy out all the shops. About thirty minutes later, I was done with moving from store to store and trying on one outfit after another. I met my mom back at the fountain where she and my sister were waiting.

"Finally," Amanda groaned when she saw me.

"Are you done with everything?" my mom asked.

"Yeah. Thanks," I said, with a smile.

"No problem. Now just watch Amanda until I get back."

"KK," I said eyeing Amanda, who was making silly faces at me.

Just like that, my mom vanished into one of the stores and I was left there with my sister.

It wasn't very long after my mom had left us when I heard Amanda say, "Hey Al isn't that Maddie with her mom?"

That's when I decided to have a look around and I saw her. Maddie.

"You know what Amanda we should get going," I told her.

"No. but mom said we should stay here and wait for her," she answered.

OMG. She was getting on my nerves. That's when I grabbed her to get us out of sight of Maddie and her mom.

"Al what are you doing?" she squeaked.

"Getting us out of here," I said getting annoyed.

"But I wanna say hi to Maddie first," she squealed.

"No, Amanda lets go," I said.

20

What Amanda did next was unexpected. She
started screaming at the top of her lungs saying
'stranger danger' on repeat.

So I obviously had to let her go.

"Sshh... Amanda what do you think you are doing!"
I whisper-shouted at her.

"I'll stop if we go over to Maddie," she said
looking up at me.

OMG. Why does the universe hate me?! (You
guys will probably get tired of me saying that,
but don't be since I'll be doing so a lot.)

"Fine let's go," I gave in.

She stopped screaming then took my hand and pulled me towards Maddie and her mom's direction. We must have looked like a dog and its owner just lazing around the mall. Only instead of me being the owner, Amanda was.

"Hi Maddie," Amanda said. She'd beamed when we'd approached them.

"Hey Amanda! Aren't you just cute," she answered.

"Hey Alize," she said and I was taken aback by surprise.

"Hi," I said looking elsewhere but her face.

"Maddie did you tell her you will both be in the same school?" her mom asked looking at the both of us.

NO. NO. NO. NO. NO.

I couldn't believe my ears. It couldn't be true. But apparently, it is.

WHY DOES THE UNIVERSE HATEE ME?

"Really?" I asked trying to sound glad to hear the news.

"Yeah," Maddie added.

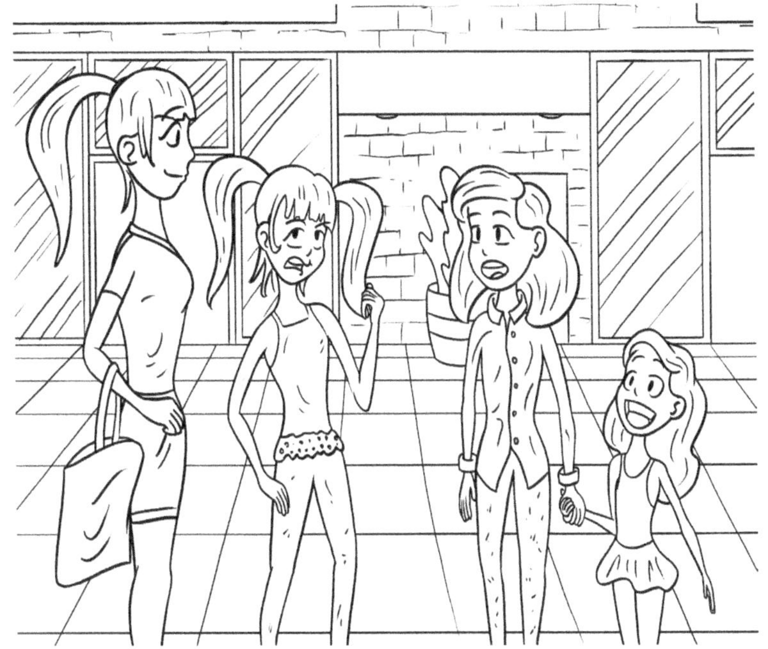

"That's great to hear. Well Amanda and I better get going," I said grabbing Amanda's hand.

"Okay, bye, take care," Maddie's mom said.

I got away from them quickly, dragging Amanda along with me. I ignored her whine to slow down and kept up the pace.

I was glad to find mom arriving at the fountain, where she told us to wait for her, the exact time we got there.

The car ride back home wasn't pleasant at all. Amanda kept on blabbing about meeting Maddie to my mom and all that.

You know there are times when you feel like you just want to disappear, well that was what I was wishing then.

A FEW SHOCKS AND SURPRISES

The day finally arrived.

THE FIRST DAY OF SCHOOL or should I say...
THE FIRST DAY OF MIDDLE SCHOOL.

I came to the conclusion that I shouldn't let
Maddie get all in my head. She's done her part
so I've decided I am going to stay bold and
positive throughout. For some reason though, it
seems that she is almost everywhere I am and
I'm pretty sure I am not wrong.

I got dressed and went downstairs to find my
mom talking to Maddie. Guess I was right when I
thought she always seemed to be everywhere I was.

"G'morning Mom," I greeted her.

"Morning sweetie," she said glancing towards me.

"Hey Maddie," I said to her.

"Hi," she said with a sense of surprise in her
tone

"Are you girls ready for school?" my mom asked.

"Yeah I've been waiting for this day for like forever,"
I answered.

"I know, I remember when you guys were young you would always talk about starting middle school together and here you are! Isn't it great?" my mom said.

"Yeah," Maddie said.

I kept quiet. All those ideas of starting middle school with Maddie changed from the day she chose to betray me. Then again, I decided I wasn't going to let her or any negative thoughts ruin my day.

"Let's go now before you two run late," my mom said rushing us out of the house.

The car ride to school was quiet. Okay, not entirely since my mom kept on ranting about her first day of middle school. As for Maddie, I could feel a couple of stares on me from time-to-time.

We finally arrived at school. It was finally real. It was a new school so that meant I was going to have to make new friends. I couldn't wait!

"Bye girls," my mom said to the both of us as we got out of the car.

"Bye," we waved as we stood on the sidewalk.

When my mom drove off, I paused for a second and

took time to glance at the building in front of me. My new school.

All the thoughts which raced across my mind brought a pleased smile across my face. And after I was ready to the enter the building, I started walking towards it. Just then -

"Alize!" Maddie called out to me.

As much as I wanted to ignore her, I was also curious to know what she wanted to say so I turned to face her.

"If you're going to apologize just forget it," I stated.

"Apologize? Why would I need to do that? All I wanted to say was that you should mind your

own business and I'll mind my own too. Basically, we should stay out of each other's way but not at home since you know our parents," she said.

I couldn't help but be surprised. How could she even say that? Who had she become? Was she the same Maddie I knew? Nope definitely not.

Again, I decided that I wouldn't let her ruin my day so I just walked away from her and went to my class.

I already knew the class I was in since I had come here last week to figure out all my class arrangement and all that. After all the searching, I finally got to my class. I walked in feeling a bit nervous with all the glares on me. Not long after Maddie came in too.

"Class, we have two more new students, Alize and Maddie," the teacher announced.

After saying that she turned to us indicating we had to introduce ourselves. It seemed like we weren't the only new students there since the teacher had said 'more'.

"Good morning everyone, my name is Alize Adler and I am thirteen years old," I said. I hoped that the teacher wouldn't ask for my middle name. BUT I jinxed it since she did.

"Do you have a middle name?" the teacher asked.

"Uhm..." I mumbled.

"No she doesn't," Maddie blurted out.

I was shocked. Why had she saved me? I'm pretty sure the others in the class were shocked too from the looks on their faces.

"Next you," the teacher pointed at Maddie.

"My name is Maddie and I am also thirteen years old. I just moved to town recently," she said.

"Okay take a seat," she said.

We took our seats and continued listening to what she was saying. She actually seemed fun.

After that class, I went outside and found Maddie already had people crowding around her.

I wasn't envious of her or anything. I just didn't like the feeling of having no friends especially at a new school where I was unfamiliar with almost everything.

I had a few other classes and then it was lunch. I still hadn't made any new friends. What cruddy luck I got. Am I right?

I took my lunch and went to sit at an empty table at the far end of the cafeteria. Just as I started eating-

"Hey is this spot free," a girl I noticed in my

class asked and I nodded.

"Why are you so quiet?" she asked looking at me.

"I don't know," I said annoyed at that question.
I hated when people asked me that.

"Okay anyway I am Brit and my friend Cindy will
be here soon," she said.

Not long after she said that, a girl came over
and sat next to her.

"So am guessing you're Cindy?" I faced her.

"Yeah hi," she said.

"Hi, and my name is Alize. I'm new here," I
introduced myself.

"Yeah I realized," she laughed out, "Nice to
meet you!"

After all the introduction, Brit, Cindy and I talked
about random stuff until it was time for our last
period.

We seemed to be getting along just fine and I
was pleased. Not bad for a first day of school.

In short, Brit is the goofy one and likes joking

around while Cindy is the opposite; let's just say she is the "mom" of the group.

Then there's me. Alize.

The day was finally coming to an end and I had a feeling Brit and Cindy would be my very good friends. In my opinion, they are just hilarious and genuine at the same time.

We walked to our last class together and sat next to each other. We didn't really do anything in that lesson except for getting to know the people around us.

It wasn't much trouble since Brit, Cindy and I pretty much already knew each other.

After that class, school was finally over. Brit, Cindy and I said our farewells to each other and went back home.

Good thing I wasn't going back with Maddie today. My dad picked me up. He asked me questions about how school was on the way back home. So I told him all about it and I got to admit, I did have a wonderful day.

Just like in *Harry Potter* it seemed like I'd found my Hermione and Ron except that Brit is a girl and Ron is a boy but you get what I mean.

2 Years Later

...

JUST KIDDING GUYS...HASN'T BEEN THAT LONG

2 Months Later

...

BACK TO WRITING

It feels like I haven't written in this diary in so long. I think I might have missed doing so. Just a tiny bit.

And - oh - look at that, I got used to calling this a diary, instead of a book.

My life has been going great these past few months, meaning Brit and Cindy are all good and we've gotten stronger than ever.

Going over to Maddie, well let's just say I rarely see her nowadays.

That's why I'm saying that my life is great and I hope it stays that way.

I wish.

Until now you guys have probably realized when anything, and I mean ANYTHING, goes right in my life, there will always be something that will go wrong.

That's a fact.

So, recently there have been posters up in school all about Halloween. Yes, that time of year where you receive and eat as much candy as you'd like. Well for some of us, not all.

This year it's going to be a bit different.

Instead of going trick or treating with my friends, I will be going to a party.

Now remember when I said there were posters in school about Halloween, well they are actually informing us about the party venues.

There were two, meaning the middle and high scholars have got separate venues.

For the middle scholars, our venue will be at Maddie's house. I'm guessing, she suggested to have the party there for popularity. BUT, no judgements. It is her choice after all.

For the high scholars, I don't really know since I didn't follow up on it. Besides it's none of my business.

The party won't just be a normal Halloween party but instead, as Maddie announced, there is going to be a costume competition.

The winners will be crowned as, 'KING HALLO and 'QUEEN WEEN. Weird names but it is what it is.

Brit, Cindy and I are really looking forward to that party and we have planned to go shopping this weekend. Our costumes have got to look bomb and fierce in order to win the thing. Now I've got my hopes up for Brit and Cindy but I'm not sure about myself.

I don't think I will win this little "competition", but it won't hurt to try out.

COSTUME SHOPPING CRISIS

My life is officially over!

So, today I asked my mom if I could get some money to go costume shopping for the Halloween Party with Brit and Cindy and she did not agree to give me any. She said and I quote,

"NO!"

Straight up, no.

She said I should've thought about it when I went shopping two months ago.

Come on! Who would even think about Halloween at that time?

I knew I couldn't cancel on Brit and Cindy just like that since they were really looking forward to the three of us going shopping together for the first time.

Anyway, I had some cash remaining from the shopping I did a while ago. I decided I would have to make the best of it.

My mom agreed to drive me to the mall but she still wouldn't lend me any money. I was grateful though since being driven was better

than nothing. I spotted Brit and Cindy just as I
entered the largest mall there was in town.
If you want to shop for anything and I mean
anything- literally. The mall has got it all.

They were psyched to see me since-

Hello, it's our first shopping together

We wanted to make memories for everything we
did for the first time. SO, we took a couple of
selfies.
As weird as we may seem, we know we are the
coolest people out there but am not saying you

guys aren't cool. In fact you all are.
Now back to the shopping.

We went around from one store to another trying
to find the best costumes. After some walking and
looking at some clothes we all finally got something to wear. I got this cute 'Queen of Hearts'
costume and I had to admit, I looked dashing.

 All was going great until I realized that I was
short of money. Brit and Cindy were sorry to
hear that. They almost wanted to give up their
costumes to get cheaper ones so I'd be able to
get mine too. Of course, I couldn't let them do
that since I'd feel a bit guilty if they did. So, I
asked them if I could use any change they received
after they bought theirs.

In the end, lucky for me, they did have some
change, so I got to buy mine too!

They truly are the best friends I could ever ask for.

After we were done with the shopping, we headed
out to get some ice cream. Since, I didn't have
any money on me Cindy bought me the ice cream
and said she wouldn't take my money if I offered
to pay her back.

Again how did I get so lucky to have them by my side?

Just as we were leaving Brit asked, " Uhm...Alize where's your costume?"

"It's here," I said lifting up a bag.

"That bag is empty Al," Cindy said.

"No it's not. See here...wait what?" I panicked.

It turned out that there was a hole right at the bottom of my bag. I had no idea how it had happened. We decided to go back to the ice-cream stand to see if the dress had accidentally dropped out there but I didn't find it.

Since it wasn't by the ice-cream stand, we decided to go back to the store I bought it in but guess what guys, IT WAS CLOSED!

Why does something have to go wrong whenever anything goes right?

Quick questions guys...

Is this normal that something has to go wrong if anything goes right? Or is it just me?

 For now am going with it's just me...what If am actually cursed or something?

The money that Brit and Cindy offered me all went to waste. Losing my costume was enough to ruin the rest of my day.

"How could I have left it in there, or worse, what if I dropped it somewhere?" I asked trying to think straight.

"It can't be gone," Brit said patting my shoulder.

"Yeah maybe you just left it in there and I can assure you they might have kept it for you," Cindy added in.

"Yeah that can be it. I'll just come here tomorrow again," I said trying to reassure myself.

"And we will be here too," Cindy said.

"You don't have to do that for me guys," I tried telling them.

"Oh we don't? Okay," Brit said and not long after received a kick from Cindy.

"I was just joking, what I meant to say is you won't be here alone," she said rolling her eyes at Cindy.

"Yeah, yeah sure," I laughed out.

"Whaat," Brit asked like a kid who's been caught

snacking on sugar.

I just shook my head because even after everything,
I knew I could always count on them.

"You guys are the best. How did I get so lucky
to have you?" I asked them smiling.

And just like that our day came to an end.
My mom had called me earlier saying that she
wouldn't be able to pick me up and that I should
go with either Brit or Cindy. Brit's mom was fine
with it so she drove me back home. In the car,
Brit dozed off and I couldn't blame her since we
had a pretty long day.

On top of that, a longer day and a costume hunt
awaits us tomorrow.

BACK AT HOME

To say I wasn't looking forward to telling my mom I lost my costume was an understatement.

Just as I opened the door I saw mom, dad, Amanda settled on the table ready for dinner with the Harrisons.

Yep that's right the Harrisons, as in Maddie's family.

"Oh you're back sweetie," Mom greeted me.

"Yeah, good evening everyone," I greeted awkwardly still in shock.

"Good evening," they all replied at different times.

"Let me take my stuff upstairs and I'll be right back," I told them.

I rushed upstairs to hide my 'costume', actually an empty bag, and returned downstairs for the unplanned dinner.

I walked to the table and sat next to Maddie.

That was the only spot left for me to sit other than the one next to Amanda - which was on the other side of the table.

"So how was shopping?" my dad asked.

"It was great," I lied.

"Can we see your costume after dinner, please?" Amanda pleaded.

"No am saving it for the day like a surprise," I said forcing a smile.

"How is school going for you guys?" Maddie's mom asked.

"Yeah did you get time to catch up," my mom chipped in.

"Uhm... I guess," I said focusing on my food.

"What she's trying to say is that school is great and yeah we did have some moments to catch up," Maddie jumped in to answer looking at me.

She is so unbelievable, like how can she just lie about that.

Now I think some of you might think, 'what's she talking about, she's also lying'. Yes, I know I'm also lying about two things now (The ones I listed below are the main ones)

1.   What really happened between Maddie and me

2.   My costume crisis.

Now you have to understand the reason as to why I lied about the costume, which is, I might be getting it back tomorrow so no need to tell them first.

On with the dinner...

"Before I forget, I'd like to know how the Halloween preparation is going so far," my mom asked both Maddie and her mom.

"We are almost done seeing the party is in a week or so," Maddie's mom replied.

After dinner was over, we all gathered in the

living room. I just sat by the corner and read this book I found on the table while Amanda was talking to Maddie. I was glad to hear when Maddie's dad finally announced it was getting late and was time for them to leave.

After everything was over I went to bed and got my peace and quiet.

I twisted and turned in bed, trying to get comfortable enough to fall asleep but I couldn't. I wondered if it was the clothes I was wearing so I decided to change into something more comfortable. It didn't help as I still couldn't fall asleep. That's when I realized that it was the sense of worry that I had which made my tummy feel queasy.

My only solution was to go downstairs to have a sip of water, and that's what I did.

"Boo!" a voice came from behind.

I jumped a little and yelped in shock.

The lights soon came on and I was startled to see my mom.

"Oh you scared me." I laughed out.

"Good to hear so which means I will be scaring a couple of people on Halloween," she joked and I laughed.

"Yeah anyway am just going to go back to sleep," I told her.

"Before you do so I'd like to ask, are you feeling okay because you have been off these past few days," she asked sounding concerned about me.

"Yeah am fine mom don't worry," I tried to reassure her.

"You sure?" she asked lifting up an eyebrow.

"Yeah positive," I said smiling.

"Okay then goodnight," she said kissing my forehead.

"G 'night," I said with a smile (willingly this time).

I went upstairs after the little talk with my mom. I felt like I needed it since I went back to sleep easily. Although I still felt bad for lying to her.

NOT SO BAD DAY

I woke up early and saying I was worried is an understatement. I couldn't stop thinking about the costume.

Thank goodness my mom didn't ask why I wanted to go back to the mall again. So, she drove me there and told me that she'd pick me up after she finished running her errands.

I arrived at the mall trying to find Cindy but not long after I received a little pat on my back.

"Oh! There you are," I squealed.

"Yeah, I've been behind you all this time and you just didn't turn around," Cindy said.

"Oh, so where's Brit?" I asked her.

"Am not sure, she's supposed to be here by now," Cindy said looking around to see if she could spot her.

"What if she overslept?" I asked.

"I hope she didn't," she said.

Just as Cindy said that Brit came rushing towards us still in her pajamas and bunny slippers. So I guess she did oversleep.

"Sorry am late guys," she apologized.

"Guessing you overslept," I laughed while eyeing her.

"Uh yeah," she said.

"OMG Brit," Cindy said shaking her head.

"Hey it's a Saturday," she pointed out.

We just laughed and made our way to the store I bought my costume at. Lucky for us the store was opened so we walked in and tried to find the guy who sold the costume to us. We couldn't find him anywhere so we just decided to go ask any random employee we could find.

"Hey excuse me, I left my costume here yesterday so any chance I could still get it?" I asked.

"Go over to the lost and found," she answered.

"Okay thanks," I replied.

"So we have to find the lost and found," I turned to tell Brit and Cindy.

"Oh, okay, lets go," Brit said.

We went over to the lost and found and I saw my costume hanging inside. I searched for the person in charge but just as I tried to get their attention... Cindy took over and spoke to her.

"Good morning, my friend left her costume here yesterday and it's that one hanging over there," she told her pointing at the costume.

"Okay, do you have the receipt with you?" she asked.

Of course, the receipt. How could I have forgotten to take it? I don't even think I have it.

"Uhm...I don't have the receipt," I whisper-shouted.

"What?! You don't," Brit asked.

"We don't have the receipt here," Cindy turned to tell the lady in charge.

"Then you will have to wait for the person who served you to get here and confirm if it is yours," she stated.

"How long do we have to wait?" I asked.

"Just about thirty minutes," she said.

"Okay thanks," we all said.

We had to wait for thirty minutes. Could this day get any worse? But luckily, Cindy suggested that we could go over to QuickDrinks, since it was nearby.

Thirty minutes went by and then we were back at that store. Thirty five minutes actually. Hey we were keeping track of the time.

We went over again to the lost and found. When the lady spotted us she soon called the guy who sold the costume to me yesterday. He came over and when he confirmed the costume belonged to me, I took it.

Before we left, Brit decided she wanted to get an outfit she could change into since she came in her pajamas after all. Cindy and I sat on the little chairs the store had while we waited for Brit to finish up. Not more than ten minutes later, Brit approached us dressed in an outfit which was way better than the pajamas and bunny slippers she had on earlier. When everything was cleared up, we exited the store.

"Let's go grab a quick lunch at RUNTOWN BURGERS then we leave," I suggested.

"Yeah let's go," both Brit and Cindy agreed.

We went to RUNTOWN BURGERS and it seemed

to be a special day for it was decorated. Brit insisted that we should all order the 'special meal' and so we did. Not long after we got our food, a shocking announcement almost made me choke on my food.

"Attention everyone! So we would like to declare table six as the winners for this little competition."

"Wait what?" both Cindy and I gasped.

"Before they claim their prize which is $30 they will have to dance to our theme song," the worker said.

Everyone was amazed by this but some were bummed that they didn't win. I was surprised that some people actually wanted to win this thing. I mean I get it if they were in it for the money but dancing in front of everyone to some childish song- that's a no no.

And to think I was called up on stage to dance to the song with Brit and Cindy.

"BRIT! Did you know about this?" I asked her.

"Maybe." She smiled.

"Just kill me right now," Cindy said.

"I can't dance," I said.

"C'mon it will be fun," Brit said.

Cindy and I gave in since we were going to get $30 afterwards and there didn't seem to be anyone we knew around.

We went on stage and some people cheered which made me feel good actually.

When the song came on, Cindy and I barely knew any of the moves. Brit was the only one who knew the moves so we did what we had to do.

Copy her.

After the song ended, we got our $30 and the restaurant manager told us that we were going to be famous after a while.

"Uhm...excuse me? How are we going to be famous exactly?" I asked.

"Oh you didn't know? The video will be uploaded on YouTube," he said.

"Y...YouTube you say?" I asked.

This is bad. I do not want to get famous this way.

"OMG Brit, did you know about this," Cindy asked in shock.

"No, and I am sorry guys I just wanted to do this real bad," Brit said.

"It's okay, you're our best friend and besides this wasn't that bad but next time please don't let us do this," I said laughing.

"Yeah I promise," she said.

After all that, we all went back home. Calling this day weird is truly an understatement.

A lot had happened and it was enough for the day.

SCHOOL TORTURE

You guys would not believe what happened at school today. It all started with a little video and I think you all remember it.

I got to school ten minutes early before school started and that was a good thing, since I would usually be late. I don't know how I even arrive late since school is just a ten-minute drive from home.

My first class was math and to all the math lovers out there, I like math too but it can be tricky sometimes.

Anyway, on with the day...

So our math teacher wanted to show us a short video on algebra and as she tapped on a video, guess what popped up...

An AD!

Now why would an AD be so bad?
Well that's because it wasn't just any AD...

It was for that place Brit, Cindy and I went to when we went to the mall. And guess what they were showing...the video of the dance we did.

Getting the video uploaded was bad enough but having it as an ad too is even worse. It was embarrassing and some people started laughing. I turned to look at Brit and Cindy to find them both with straight faces.

As soon as class ended I went over to Brit and Cindy and we all got out of that class before anyone brought up the video.

We were sitting at lunch when a couple of jocks came over to the table and imitated the dance right in front of us.

Some people have just got the nerve...

"Hey don't you have somewhere else to go?" I snapped.

Okay, I wasn't going to let anyone torment us.

Yes, we did the dance and so what. You know what? I am going to be proud of that video. Well not entirely, just when people make fun of us.

"Oh! But isn't that how you guys were dancing," said one of the annoying boys, assuming he was the captain.

"Just leave if you don't have anything important to do here," I said.

"Yeah just leave," Brit chipped in.

They left. Looks like we really took them down.

"Brit I just wanted to say you looked great in that video," one of the jocks said when the others were gone.

That statement made Brit blush like crazy.

"Thanks," she said, smiling really big.

"Anytime," he said back with a wink, then he left.

"Briittt," I said eyeing her.

"Brit he's totally into you," Cindy said with excitement.

"Yeah, he really is and what's his name," I asked.

"Matt," Brit said, acting like it's not a big deal.

"As you say so but I just saw love in the air for a second there," I added looking at my food with a smirk.

That made me receive a gentle shove from her.

"Oh, fine am just kidding...not," I said whispering the last part just loud enough for Cindy to hear.

She just looked and smiled at me.

"Now time for the last class," I said.

"Yeah and we have gone through this day without anyone mentioning the video except for those guys," Cindy stated.

After that we just went to our last class. I won't get into detail since nothing interesting really happened.

 When the class was over Brit, Cindy and I were standing outside class talking for a while when Maddie and her group of friends approached us.

"Well, well, well if it isn't the school's little celebrities," Maddie said as she came over to us with her hands crossed.

Brit, Cindy and I all turned to face her.

"Looks like your little video is trending nowadays and you are the celebs of the school am I right?" she said.

Some people in her group laughed at the joke, which I didn't find funny.

I whispered to Brit and Cindy that it would be best to just walk away.

Just as we started to walk away -

"Oh, look they are scared," one of the girls said and that caught me off guard.

"Now look here, we aren't scared but we don't have time for this nonsense," I said and got a squeeze from Cindy telling me to chill.

"Let's just go guys," Cindy said.

"No fun in that," another of them said.

A few of the guys were passing by so Maddie pointed at us to grab even more attention.

Anyway the guys came up and started doing our so called famous dance. To make it even worse they had the song on too.

I was going to lose my temper real soon if they didn't stop.

I could see Brit's glance on Matt who thank goodness wasn't dancing with them. Brit expected Matt to stop them and just as we thought he wouldn't -

"Guys stop. This isn't cool," he said and they all stopped.

"He so likes you," I said.

"I don't know about that," she said smiling.

"He told his squad to stop for you," Cindy pointed out.

"Yeah, so why would he do it if he didn't like you and did you see the wink and smile he gave you," I said and later on got a kick from her.

By the time we got to the parking lot, I could see my mom waiting so I just said my goodbyes to Cindy and Brit and left.

Okay today wasn't so bad like I tried to make it sound in the beginning. I stood up against Maddie, her friends and the football jocks. And most importantly, discovered young love between Brit and Matt.

NEXT BORING DAYS

After what happened yesterday, nothing was interesting at school except for the learning we had. Brit continued acting weird around Matt and you could obviously tell they liked each other.

The Halloween party is this week Friday. With three days left, everyone is psyched about it.

For real, almost everywhere you go in school you would hear people saying, 'I can't wait for the Halloween party' or 'what are you wearing' and 'I hope I win'.

Well you get it, people are excited about this and I can't say that am not because I am. Brit, Cindy and I decided we would get ready at my house, since my house is closer to Maddie's.

It had been announced that the Halloween party would be as follows:

Everyone wishing to participate in the contest would have a quick show of their costume. At each stage the ones who won't be participating could cast their vote. After that, the judges would decide the winners to be crowned. The aim for this party wasn't to compete but rather enjoy ourselves. The little contest was just an add-on to the party.

If Brit, Cindy or I get lucky to end up getting crowned, I will be extremely happy. I can already picture Maddie's reaction in my mind, if it would end up happening.

Or imagine if Brit and Matt get crowned king and queen then they would get their own dance in the spotlight. I hope it happens since Brit's costume surely is a winner and no doubt about Matt's either.

Anyway, enough about this party...

I'll just stop writing in here until Friday, since that's when things will be interesting again.

SATURDAY
Sorry guys I forgot to fill you in yesterday night and now I forgot almost everything that happened!!!

JOKINGGG!!

IT'S FINALLY FRIDAY...NOW TUNE IN THE NEXT PAGES FOR SOME TEA - HOPE ITS GOOOD.

DAY OF THE HALLOWEEN PARTY

This is probably going to be the longest diary entry I've written so far.

I'm going to start from the part when school ended, because I don't think you would want to know what I learned in my classes. All I can say is everything was great except for the maths pop quiz we had. Even though I think I will ace it, I still needed the heads up about it so I could've gotten my brain activated.

The final bell had just rang when Brit, Cindy and I were in the parking lot waiting for mom to pick us up.

"My mom's taking forever," I whined.

"Yeah, I am tired of standing here," Brit said wiggling her feet.

"Hmm... maybe she's just caught up in traffic jam," Cindy said.

"I guess so," I said and caught sight of Matt coming towards us.

"Brit! Matt's coming over!" I whisper-shouted and she turned and caught glimpse of him too.

"OMG! What should I do," she said, kind of freaking out.

"Just act normal," Cindy said laughing at her.

"Hey guys," Matt said as he approached us.

"Hey," we all said at once.

"So Brit can I talk to you for a sec," Matt asked waiting for her reply.

"Uhh... sure," she hesitated.

They went a short distance away from us. Of course that didn't stop Brit and I from spying on them. Even though we were out in the open, it still counted as spying to me.

"OMG what do you think they're talking about," I asked Cindy, going crazy.

"You know we are getting excited while Brit should be the one who should be," Cindy said.

"Yeah that's true but who cares." I laughed.

"Here she comes," Cindy pointed out and we both ran to her.

"So?" Both Cindy and I asked her looking at her.

"He just asked me if I could save him a dance and I said yes!" she squealed.

"Aaahhhh," we all screamed jumping up and down.

"That's great!" I squealed.

"Yeah and here comes your mom," she said.

"About time but good thing she was late or this wouldn't have happened," I pointed out as we walked towards the car.

"Yeah it's like this was destined to be," Cindy said.

"Oh stop it you two," she said rolling her eyes.

We finally got into the car and my mom apologized for being late. Turns out she really was caught up in a traffic jam.

The car ride was a bit boring since both Brit and Cindy were asleep.

"Alize, I'll need you, Brit and Cindy to take Amanda to the park when we get back," she announced.

"Mom, no! Why?" I asked not liking the sudden change in our plans.

"I can't take her because I have to get back to work and please just do it. She will only be there for an hour," she said looking at.me.

"Ohh, okay that's fine," I said.

I shook Brit and Cindy to wake them up to tell them about the news.

"Really that's nice," Cindy exclaimed.

"Yeah I can't wait to play with the little kids at the park," Brit gushed.

"Why is Amanda going there again mom?" I asked her.

"She has a Halloween party even though it's going to be a bit early. They decided to do it that way since they're young and can't stay up late at night partying," she explained.

"Ohh," I said, understanding everything now.

So instead of Brit, Cindy and I watching Netflix as we had planned, we will be watching over my little sister at a Halloween party.

Just great.

Not long after we pulled up in our driveway, Brit, Cindy and I rushed upstairs to get changed.

After changing we were faced by a 'vampire' who apparently was my sister in her costume. I had to admit she looked great with the light makeup mom did to her.

"Brit! Cindy! And Alize," she exclaimed hugging both Brit and Cindy.

"It looks cute," she said admiring her.

This girl...she just said Brit and Cindy's names all excited except mine but I could honestly care less.

"How's my costume," she asked turning around.

"It's good and you truly look like a vampire," Brit pointed out.

"I have to admit Amanda, the costume looks amazing on you," I said with a smile.

"Thank you guys," she smiled and hugged all of us this time.

"Okay we should get going to the park now," I said since we already wasted plenty of time.

We left and headed to the park. It took us seven minutes to get there, not bad, but we had to listen to Amanda talk about the Halloween party all the way.

As soon as we got there, Amanda rushed to her friends and ditched us, just like that.

"So basically, what are we supposed to do while we wait?" I turned to ask Brit and Cindy to find them already playing with some kids.

Okay, so I think I was the only one not psyched about the whole idea of staying at the park.

I guess I could just go with the flow and play around with these kids.

"Alize?" one kid called me.

I turned to see who it was to find out it was Maddie's cousin Mads, short for Madeline. She used to go over to Maddie's house for any holidays she had.

Amanda and Mads have been best friends ever since they met even though they don't get to see each other frequently.

"You've grown so much," I said trying to carry her.

"Yeah and I've missed you so much. I haven't seen you in like two years or so," she said hugging me.

"Yeah and I missed you too," I said.

"Did anything happen between you and Maddie because every time I try asking her about you she says she doesn't want to talk about it," she asked.

"Uhh...nothing really happened. We just haven't hung out in a while," I answered.

"Okay and I am coming over to your house for a sleepover since the Halloween party is at Maddie's house," she said.

"That's great and yeah I can't wait for the party," I said.

"Okay well am going to get back to my friends now. It was nice talking to you," she said and ran back to the other kids.

The party was soon over before I realized and we were off again back home. This time Mads was with us.

Now that I think of it, both Maddie and Madeline have the same nicknames, Mads. Okay guys I have to stop writing now because am tired out.

Imagine going to a party late at night then coming back home all tired out. My eyes can barely open at the moment so I will just stop here for now.

DAY OF THE HALLOWEEN PARTY CONT...

Okay so where did I end yesterday?

Hmm... so we were heading back home from Amanda's Halloween party. When we got home, we still had two more hours until the party would officially start.

We decided to take a short nap to be fully prepared for the party.

By the time we woke up, we only had less than an hour to get ready and leave.

We took it in turns to use the shower and later on got dressed in our costumes.

I dressed up as the queen of hearts, for all the people who know her.

Brit dressed up as a mummy and I have to say she really looked great.

Cindy dressed up as an angel- yep simple costume but it suited her.

Before we left the house my mom suggested to take a pic of us, for memories people.

She said since it was our first Halloween party together we had to capture the moment.

We rushed out of the front door and walked into Maddie's house. The party was already looking lit with the songs blasting through the speakers.

"Let's do this," I said at the front door to Cindy and Brit.

We walked in to find people dancing, some talking and the others just stuffing their faces. I almost forgot that we also took pictures before entering the party.

A few moments in the party Brit had gone into dance with Matt. Cindy and I were by the punch bowl refilling our cups. Unsurprisingly, Maddie came over to us with her new best friend.

"Oh you came! And I love that costume of yours," Maddie gushed.

"Uhh...yeah everyone was invited," I said.

"Okay let's go Eve," she said and walked past us when -

"OMG I am so sorry," she apologized with no empathy.

I was still tongue tied in shock and Cindy was trying to see what had just happened.

"My costume," I said since it was the only thing I could actually speak out.

"Oh no I am so sorry again, now your costume is ruined. Poor you. You can't participate in the contest now. Oh, what a bummer," she said with a smile plastered across her face.

I was so mad at her at that time. I couldn't even say anything because I didn't expect the incident to happen.

"Let's just go try and get this cleaned up," Cindy said pulling my arm.

Not knowing what to do anymore, I just followed her straight to the bathroom. Brit must have seen us rushing to the bathroom looking worried so she came in too.

"What happened?" she asked stunned.

"Maddie," I said. "Now my costume is ruined and I won't be able to win or anything." I sighed.

"I'm sorry that this happened Al but at least the party was fun," Cindy said trying to cheer me up.

"Yeah you shouldn't let her put you down okay and besides it doesn't matter if you don't win," Brit said and I let out a deep sigh.

"Uh huh, just as long as we all have fun," Cindy added.

After all that pep talk, I decided to go out and enjoy the party.

Not long after...

"Attention everyone! It's time to crown the king and queen so everybody gather up," a teacher announced.

Everyone went around the stage eager to know the winners.

"Okay, so we are going to start with the king Halo who is... can you all guess?" the teacher asked. and everyone cheered.

"ZACH!" the crowd yelled.

"Indeed it is, Zach is our King Halo!" he finally announced.

I wasn't surprised because his costume was pretty cool and in fact he was kind of popular, one of the jocks let's say.

"And our Queen Ween for tonight is the one and only..." the teacher was saying.

"Maddie," I said guessing it was her.

"ALIZE!" she said.

'What?' 'OMG' was all I heard from Brit and Cindy since I was zoned in the moment as I walked up to stage and met my 'king'.

We headed to the dance floor and we danced with the spotlight and most of the people's eyes on us.

After the dance, Zach ended with, "See you around." Just like that.

Back in reality, I still could not believe I was crowned queen. My costume was ruined so how did I?

Cindy and Brit kept on talking about Maddie's reaction when she heard that I was the one who won.

Guess her plan to make me loose just did not work out.

For a girl whose costume was sabotaged, not bad. HA! Take that Maddie. I beat her at her own game.

Anyway, the only reason I won was because the pictures we took at the entrance were the ones being judged. The judges had predicted anything could have happened during the party to ruin the costume, just like what happened to me.

Brit, Cindy and I decided to just hang around for some time. Basically, that was how the Halloween party turned out for me. In my point of view, I'd say it was the best party I have ever been to- or should I say for my first ever party it was great!

When I went back home my mom was surprised and very happy that I actually won. And yes, she took a pic of me in the costume with the crown. Even though the stain was still there, the pic turned out perfect.

Perfect enough for me.

FAREWELLS AND GOODBYES

Before I say anything, I just felt the need to say that farewell and goodbye is actually the same thing. Okay, I don't see the point of saying that but let me continue with my farewells.

Thank you all for reading my diary of my super boring life, as I think of it, but you guys didn't think my life was boring and I appreciate it so much.

A lot has happened during these first few months from Maddie moving in town again to me being crowned QUEEN WEEN like how amazing is that.

I mean the part when I was crowned queen not when Maddie moved in. Even after all this had happened I still managed to have a happy ending. I mean being crowned Queen Ween is a big thing.

So then use this story of my life as an example for whenever anyone tries to go all out of their way to make you fail.

I don't really care about Maddie anymore, since I have got my two besties or let's say Ron and Hermione for all the Harry Potter fans out there.

Having Brit and Cindy is awesome; they are always there for me and we stick with each other through thick and thin.

To add on that, I am officially out of school for
two weeks.

YAY!

It won't even matter if I get excited anyway
since I have nothing planned to do.

Literally.

EXTRA (CHARACTERS INFO)

ALIZE- ME.

BRIT AND CINDY (BSFs).

MOM AND DAD (PARENTS BUT IT'S OBVIOUS).

AMANDA (LIL SIS).

MADDIE (FRENEMY, nicest way to say it).

MADDIE'S MOM AND DAD (OKAY ANOTHER OBVIOUS ONE MADDIE'S PARENTS).

MATT (hint: Brit).

JOCKS (FOOTBALL/SOCCER PLAYERS AT SCHOOL).

Before you finish up, have a go at this quick word search to see how many words you can find!

For an extra challenge, feel free to do it under three minutes :)

Now, HURRY! Time's running out...

W	B	M	A	D	D	I	E	A	K
Q	U	E	E	J	K	Y	U	I	I
S	S	Q	K	G	L	V	N	E	S
F	X	F	Y	Q	M	G	X	W	L
I	W	E	P	W	H	I	C	Z	C
U	P	L	Q	A	A	Q	X	C	I
Q	B	C	L	S	L	T	E	H	N
U	I	O	R	A	L	I	Z	E	D
E	S	E	Z	E	O	S	G	D	Y
E	W	R	Q	A	W	F	S	L	B
N	V	U	J	M	E	L	F	X	R
W	B	T	K	U	E	Q	M	P	I
E	E	R	B	A	N	H	N	O	A
E	H	O	E	R	D	L	D	C	S
N	L	T	L	T	I	R	B	Z	R

ALIZE	QUEENWEEN
BCA	HALLOWEEN
BRIT	MADDIE
CINDY	TRAUMA
KINGHALO	TORTURE

AUTHOR BIOGRAPHY

Teen **Doreen Ngemera** was born and raised in the busy City of Dar es Salaam, Tanzania by her pharmacist dad and medical doctor mum alongside her two siblings. She spent her childhood reading and reviewing all sorts of diaries and novels. By the age of 10 she had already read more than 500 fiction and non-fiction books. While reading the books the passion and fire of writing emerged in her heart. As a result, Doreen participated and won more than 10 medals related to creative writing and debating in a globally recognized competition - the **World Scholar's Cup®**. She remains one of the very few teen writers in the African continent. Of course, she considers herself born to inspire.

www.ingramcontent.com/pod-product-compliance
Lightning Source LLC
Chambersburg PA
CBHW070451170726
48291CB00005B/1701